STREET HEROES
RUNAWAYS

For Ahn Chol

Text copyright © Joe Layburn 2011
Illustrations copyright © John Williams 2011
The right of Joe Layburn to be identified as the author and John Williams to be
identified as the illustrator of this work has been asserted by them in accordance with
the Copyright, Designs and Patents Act, 1988 (United Kingdom).

First published in Great Britain and the USA in 2011 by
Frances Lincoln Children's Books, 4 Torriano Mews,
Torriano Avenue, London NW5 2RZ
www.franceslincoln.com

A catalogue record for this book is available from the British Library.

ISBN 978-1-84780-080-0

Set in Bembo

Printed in Croydon, Surrey, UK by CPI Bookmarque Ltd. in November 2010
1 3 5 7 9 8 6 4 2

STREET HEROES
RUNAWAYS

JOE LAYBURN

Illustrated by John Williams

F

FRANCES LINCOLN
CHILDREN'S BOOKS

OMAR

When I first heard his voice, late that autumn night, my nerves were already messed up. Whitechapel High Street, eleven o'clock. A drunken old tramp had just lurched across the pavement towards me like a wild-eyed zombie. There was even a ghostly mist in the damp East London air. It felt as if I was walking through the set of a cheap horror film.

My name is Jack. I know that you can hear me. Please be afraid!

It was someone's idea of a joke. Nothing to get freaked out about. That's what I told myself, anyway.

Remember, I've been hearing voices all my life, starting with my sister Fatima's. She has always been able to read my mind, share her thoughts with me, even when we are far apart. But this wasn't a child's voice or even a young person's. It was deep and strange, and 'Jack' was using Fatima's trademark greeting.

I said, I know that you can hear me, Omar.

I actually swung around to check if he was behind me, even though I knew this was a 'thought-voice'. When you're telepathic, you get used to people dropping into your brain for a chat. They're usually friendly. You hardly ever feel threatened by them.

I began walking faster, cursing my father and his forgetfulness. It was his fault that I was out on the streets at all. How many times had he left his glasses at home? And how often had I been called to bring them to our uncle's restaurant so my father could see well enough to sort out the evening's takings?

You seem afraid, Omar, and I like that. You should be scared of me.

2

I decided to ignore him and his weird, mocking voice. But it's not easy to block people's thoughts. Jack knew that I could hear him. If you try to screen out a thought-voice, it's like not picking up the phone when someone knows you're at home.

I won't be ignored, Omar. That's one thing I cannot stand. I've been around a long time. And people take notice of me.

I'd reached the neon-lit street in Bangla Town where my uncle's restaurant jostled for business alongside all the others. At last I could start to relax. My father wasn't telepathic, nor was my mother or my big brother Sadiq. But they knew about Fatima and me, and what my father called our 'gift'. I would tell my father about the creepy voice I'd been hearing and ask if I could wait to walk home with him.

Of course, it's your sister I'm most interested in, Omar. I've never liked goodness. It's always brought out the worst in me.

I clenched my jaw, my fists. No one threatened my sister - I'd merk them if they

dared. But suddenly, I was flying through the foggy night, sent sprawling by a black bin-liner full of rubbish.

I rubbed the pavement grit off the palms of my hands. The fall had ripped the cloth of my trousers and my left knee was grazed. As I got up, I glanced into a shadowy alley that ran down the side of an off-licence. What I saw there made me shiver. Looming out of the darkness was a tall figure. I could not make out his features, but he was beckoning me towards him with long, bony fingers.

"Come and help me, there's a good boy. I just need a bit of change if you've got any on yer."

I laughed out loud. It was just another old tramp begging for money. I felt relieved, as well as stupid for letting myself get so worked up. That's when I heard Jack's voice again.

Look further down, Omar, past the old fool and the dustbins. It's dark, isn't it? But can you see me? I won't stay in the shadows forever, Omar. This is just the beginning. Even I don't know where it will end.

For a second, I felt too frozen to move. I was afraid for myself and scared for the old tramp too.

"Get out of there, you're in danger!" I screamed. Then, without looking back, I ran.

GEORGIE

He kicked me so hard I lost a tooth. He kicked me because he was drunk. He kicked me, as I lay sleeping, because he knew he could get away with it.

It wasn't a dream. I didn't wake up in my nice warm bed. I woke up terrified and cold. I'm always cold.

When he kicked me, I was lying under a blanket on a flattened out cardboard box. I looked like rubbish. He was dressed to kill: sharp suit, shiny black shoes - a young City worker with short, brown hair and flushed cheeks.

Perhaps he'd had a bad day, lost his firm some money, been turned down by one of the secretaries he fancied. Whatever, he took it out on me: kicked me in the head, then ran off, shouting, into the night.

I'm Georgie Smith. Unless you've been living in a cave in Afghanistan or a crater on the moon, you'll have heard of me. You'll also know George Smith, my dad. He's the former leader of the British Fascist Party. He's the man who wanted to march with his followers down Cable Street in East London and terrorise the Muslims who live there. He's the loser who was turned back by a bunch of kids – well, about a thousand of them, actually, but kids even so.

I was there that day. I stood shoulder to shoulder with those kids and helped to destroy him. Thanks to me – his 'son and heir' – George Smith is a broken man, despised by all the Nazis who used to support him. He's also loathed by those people who never liked him anyway. I suppose I still love him. Despite everything, he's my dad. But none of that matters now.

After our victory in Cable Street, one of the newspapers called us 'Street Heroes' for standing up to the fascists. I don't feel much like a hero and I don't expect a hero's welcome if I ever do go home.

I've stayed away for nearly five weeks now. It's easier than you might think for a teenage runaway to simply disappear. I haven't tried to contact my mum, or Albion, my sister. I suppose I'm starting to see my family as part of my old life.

Where my new life will take me, I don't yet know. I'm just trying to survive. When you live on the streets, that's the best you can hope for.

MELISSA

Fatima has become totally obsessed with street children. She tells me about these kids living on rubbish dumps in Brazil who got 'disappeared' when the authorities decided to clean up the big cities for the tourists. By 'disappeared' she means murdered.

I say to her, "How could they get away with killing kids?"

She says, "There are places you wouldn't believe, Melissa. Places that are very different from here."

She goes on and on about this street kid from North Korea, a girl called Hyun-mi. According to Fatima, North Korea is this scary, closed-off country near China that's run by a madman. He's let millions of his people starve to death and put thousands of them in prison. Fatima tells me it's going to be her 'life's work' to make Hyun-mi's story known to a 'global audience'.

I say, "I thought what we did to George Smith in Cable Street was your life's work."

But it seems Saint Fatima has plans for more good deeds.

I shouldn't joke about her. I know how special she is. She may be blind, but she can tune in to a million different people's thought-waves - mine included, which is why I have to be careful what I think if I don't want a pinch on the arm. She gets a lot of her information from the computer in her bedroom which talks to her day and night in this robot voice. But being telepathic means that, even without the internet, Fatima can plug in to a network of minds all over the world.

I'm pretty sure her new obsession started because of Georgie. Since Cable Street, he's been sleeping rough. He's had a hard time on the streets of our own city and she's worried about him. But her concern never stops with just one person. Fatima won't rest until this whole messed-up world is a better place, especially for kids.

"Why don't they show stuff about street children on television, Melissa? You tell me that," she says.

I look at her guiltily because I usually only watch rubbish on TV. This is one of those questions where she doesn't really want me to answer. I say nothing.

"It's because the television companies make easy money from crap like *Celebrity Skin*, even though, deep down, they must know they could do so much good with their programmes."

She throws up her hands like a magician releasing a dove. Fatima hardly ever uses bad language, but *Celebrity Skin*, with its one-hit pop singers in bikinis and nearly-naked soap stars, really annoys her. It's filmed in a compound in Docklands, just a few miles from her house, and she keeps threatening to go there and burn it to the ground.

"I thought you disagreed with violence," I say. "I thought your hero Gandhi was all about 'passive resistance'."

She pinches my arm.

"For *Celebrity Skin* I'd make an exception. Probably even Gandhi would."

HYUN-MI

The icy water almost makes me gasp. I stop myself, though. I know I must stay silent if I am to survive this night – no splashing, coughing, or cursing the cold. I wade a few steps, then push off from the rocky bottom and start swimming with slow, careful strokes towards the other side of the river.

Unlike most people in my country, I learnt to swim in a proper pool. There were other luxuries too: embroidered dresses, music and dance lessons. But that all changed. One day my father was an important man, trusted by the Dear Leader himself, the next he was dragged off to a prison camp. Now I'm leaving North Korea with nothing but the ragged clothes I am wearing.

I've seen the Tumen River on maps at school, spoken about to it to the orphan children I've met on the streets of our towns and villages. It's not that wide, not that fast flowing, but it's often deadly for North Koreans who try to escape.

This is my country's border with China and I, Hyun-mi, am finally swimming across it! My hands and feet are getting numb, but cramp is only one of my worries. If the North Korean guards who patrol the river see me, they will shoot without thinking. If I am picked up on the Chinese side I'll be sent back to a North Korean prison camp, maybe to die there like my father.

Luckily for me, the night is dark and starless. Pollution from the factories on the Chinese side of the river makes sure of that. But no North Korean is truly lucky, apart from the Dear Leader that is.

It seems strange to have to tell anyone about the Dear Leader. Everyone in my country knows him as a god. His picture hangs alongside that of his long dead father, the Great Leader, in every home, school and workplace. In the streets and squares, their statues watch over us too. They give you the creeps once you realise they're not gods. Not kind gods, anyway.

If you talk to the truly brainwashed people like my grandmother, they will say that the Dear Leader is more handsome than any film star, that he is our cleverest mathematician, our most brilliant scientist, our bravest soldier. They will coo like doves about how he loves us, his people. The truth is he loves only himself. And he doesn't look like a film star either. Our Dear Leader is fat, with horrible, wiry, brushed-back hair and big round glasses that make him look like a confused old owl. That he stayed so fat when millions of his people were dying of starvation tells you much more about him than my grandmother's fairy stories.

I've been swimming for what feels like ages,

but the other side of the river seems to get no closer. My strokes are becoming tired and erratic now and I keep swallowing great gulps of river water. I start to panic. I've travelled so many miles to get here. Am I really going to drown within yards of freedom? Then I hear the border guards' cries from behind me.

"Hey you, come back here!"

"Stop, now, or we will shoot!"

A torch beam swings across the water just to my right and a single rifle shot rings out. Then I hear the coaxing, encouraging voice of my faraway thought-friend, the one who's been with me throughout my escape.

Stay strong, Hyun-mi. You must keep going. You've come so far and now you're almost there.

It is Fatima. I fill my lungs with the chill night air then dive beneath the water, kicking my legs dolphin-tail-style, as I've been taught. When I surface, I hear another rifle shot. The bullet zings through the air close above me. I feel like shouting back at them that they must be mad to stay in North Korea. Why don't they put down their guns and join me? But no doubt these are true believers, probably boys, not much older than me, who remain devoted to the Dear Leader.

Finally, I stretch down my toes and realise I can touch the bottom. Crouching low, still shivering with terror and cold, I wade to the bank then scramble up it into some scraggy bushes.

China, at last! Lying exhausted on my back I look up into the dark night sky. I'm still not safe, but I've escaped the great prison that is the country of my birth. Despite my fear, I feel the muscles of my face form themselves into a smile.

"I'm coming to you Fatima," I whisper. "You promised we would meet one day and I've never doubted you for a second."

GEORGIE

When you live on the streets, it can seem like everyone's staring at you. I get really paranoid. I worry that some do-gooder will call the police and they'll try to send me home. I'm jumpy every time I see a uniform - even if it's just a traffic warden's.

Mostly, though, street children are made to feel like they're invisible. If you haven't got money for food, you end up begging. That's when you start to doubt you even exist. People look away from you, cross the road to avoid you.

Some of the homeless kids I've got to know will sit all day near cashpoints, mumbling the

words I'm so sick of saying – "Spare us some change, please?"

Sometimes they do all right. Often they'll get nothing.

One drizzly evening, I was sitting by a cashpoint in Soho with my blanket round my knees and a McDonald's cardboard cup clasped in my hands. It was empty except for a few coppers and a ten pence coin. Two youngish women came towards me, teetering on high heels and wearing what my mum would call their 'glad rags'.

"You look freezing," the blonde one said. "Are you all right?"

Her dark-haired friend barely glanced at me. She fumbled in her designer handbag and pulled a bank card from her purse.

"There's no point giving him money, Ange, he'll only spend it on drugs."

I wanted to tell her she was wrong – that I didn't take drugs, that I was dry-mouthed and dizzy with hunger. But what was the use? People don't believe a word you say when your face is unwashed and your clothes are dark with grime.

The cash machine was spitting out notes as though the dark haired woman had won some huge prize. She sorted them into a fat wedge, then bent down to squint at me. Her eyelashes were so thick with mascara they made me think of spiders crawling through black paint. Her Ferrari-red lips were thin and unsmiling.

She waved the wad of money under my nose.

"Listen. The reason I've got this is cos I work hard. I don't sit on my backside and beg off of other people. You should get a job, you little sponger."

The blonde woman, Ange, put a hand on her shoulder.

"Leave him, Cathy. How can he get a job? He can't be more than fifteen."

The dark haired one straightened up.

"Well, what about his family? They should look after him, not leave it to the rest of us."

I wanted to tell her that, as cold and

miserable as I was, I would rather take my chances living rough than go home. That was true of all the long-time street kids I'd met. The homes they were running from were even worse than the dark, dangerous streets they kept running to. Imagine your mum's a drug addict and her new boyfriend has threatened to kill you. Or let's say your dad is the most hated man in Britain. You might feel the same.

The blonde woman was opening her own purse now. She took out a two pound coin which flashed silver and gold under the street lights, like pirate's treasure.

"Don't take no notice of her, she's had a bad day. You buy yourself a Big Mac with this."

She gave me the money and a strained little smile.

"But promise, darling, not booze or drugs."

I started to speak, but she'd already turned away.

The pair of them clattered off down the road in search of some pub or wine bar where they would no doubt drink till they were 'off their faces'. That was one of my dad's expressions, but I decided to put any thought of him straight out of my mind.

Not that there was much room there suddenly.

You know the feeling you get when someone's watching you? When you're telepathic, you sense if people are tuning in to your thoughts, earwigging on your private conversations.

I had that feeling now and it made me nervous. Whoever it was had not bothered to announce themselves in the usual friendly way. They were just lurking beneath the surface of my mind like a crocodile in a pool.

Finally, he spoke. It was a strange voice, deep and brooding.

She shouldn't have talked to you like that, Georgie. Women like her have got no class.

Who are you? I asked.

I felt queasy suddenly. My temples throbbed.

You can call me Jack, like Jack the Ripper, he said. *I'm hoping very much that we will soon be able to meet.*

MELISSA

"So, who is this Jack the Ripper?" I asked Fatima.

"Well, unless he's come back from the dead, he's not the serial killer from Victorian times who murdered women all around Whitechapel."

I shuddered. Fatima really knew how to spook me out.

"Seriously, you think some serial killer has come back to life?"

She did that thing she does with her hands where it looks like she's throwing confetti up into the air.

"Melissa, you exasperate me. You've watched so much rubbish on those cable TV channels it's messed up your head."

I just smiled. I never minded Fatima teasing me. Now that we were real friends – not just thought-friends – and I was round her house all the time, I felt so happy. There wasn't anything she could have said that would have made me slip back into my bad old ways. At school, though, I still hadn't lost my reputation for what Kele in our class called "amazing acts of violence and destruction".

"Innit, you're worried about Georgie?" I said.

"Of course I am. It's been so hard for him on the streets. And now there's this Jack..."

"So why don't you just tell his dad where he is and he can pick him up?"

She frowned and it was like a little cloud had passed across the sun.

"Melissa, you're not to let Georgie know that his father phoned me. If they are ever to be reconciled, Georgie must find his own way back to him."

"It's not like you can be there to stop bad stuff happening to him, though."

"Melissa, I trust Georgie to keep himself safe. He's an amazing boy. Brave and resourceful."

I just clicked my tongue.

"But you did sort of lie to Georgie's dad. He thinks that Georgie is staying with people you know."

"I didn't say *staying* with. I said he's being *looked after* by someone I know."

"Yeah, but what if this Jack is pure evil? Like, there's a programme I saw where this vampire can shape-shift and one minute he's like a raven, or a crow or something and then he's a bat, but always he's this totally evil super spirit and there's no good in him at all and no human can ever fight against him."

Fatima shook her head slowly.

"Melissa, there is a lot of evil in this world and it's done by human beings, not by vampires who can turn into blackbirds. Human beings can be stopped."

"I said raven or crow, not blackbird."

"OK, Melissa, whatever."

HYUN-MI

I've actually met the Dear Leader in the flesh, or "in the flab", as my father put it. My father was his personal doctor - well, one of a whole team of them. The Dear Leader's health was far too important to be entrusted to just one physician.

Because my father travelled with the Dear Leader on his endless trips around the country - inspecting our million-strong army, visiting factories and farms - he got to see what was really going on in North Korea. He also got to see the Dear Leader in his underpants.

"Doctors are forced to look at sights that

no mortal should have to see," he'd tell me with a wink.

If you talked to my grandmother about the Dear Leader's physique, she would giggle like a young girl and wave her bony hands around like fluttering birds.

"Oh, he must be a weightlifter, he's so muscular and strong. And you know he is our country's greatest ever boxer. He once went into a ring with the nation's ten best fighters and beat them all at once."

When grandmother babbled on like this, my father would put down the medical book he was reading.

"Stop filling the girl's head with nonsense, Mother. He's a fat old fool who couldn't even win a fight against you. In any case, he's got a heart condition, though I admit it was a considerable surprise to me to find he actually has a heart."

Grandmother would simply listen to this blasphemous talk then give a toothless smile. As much as she idolised the Dear Leader, she loved my father more.

"Your father is such a joker," she would tell me. "Next he will try to tell you that our Dear Leader is not the world's greatest golfer."

She smiled sweetly at my father.

"He is *not* the world's greatest golfer, Mother. Do you have any idea how rare it is in golf to shoot a hole in one, yet our Dear Leader claims to score three or four of them every time he plays."

"It shows how fine an athlete he is."

"It shows that he's a liar and the people he surrounds himself with are too scared to contradict him."

Grandmother suddenly looked serious. Her paper-thin skin was still smooth despite her age, but she was frowning now.

"You would be wise to stay in his favour yourself, dearest one."

It made me wonder if other families in Pyongyang, our capital city, ever had such conversations. Were they too frightened to criticise Comrade Kim Jong-il, the Dear Leader, in case the secret police kicked in their doors and dragged them off to prison? Or did they just believe all the propaganda, however unbelievable it seemed?

Of course, I knew well enough never to say bad things about Kim Jong-il in public. I'd always join in when the children at my school were praising his superhuman feats. And no one sang more lustily than me when it was time for a chorus of *No Motherland Without You*, our country's favourite song. You really want to hear it?

Even if the world changes hundreds of times,
People believe in you, Comrade Kim Jong-il,
We cannot live without you,
Our country cannot exist without you,
Oh. . . Our comrade Kim Jong-il,
Our country cannot exist without you.

You could never get away from that awful tune. It blared from loudspeakers on the city streets. Every night it would sound from televisions in the Pyongyang apartments where

I and the rest of the country's elite lived our fortunate lives. By fortunate, I mean compared to everyone else in North Korea. But we were far from free.

OMAR

I can totally see why Sadiq freaked out. He was upstairs in our bedroom, supposedly doing his coursework for uni, but really just daydreaming and staring out of the window. Suddenly two police cars pulled up on the street below and guess who got out of one of them? None other than George Smith, the ex-leader of the British Fascist Party – the man Sadiq and his former friends once plotted to kill. My big brother's terrorist mates had fled the country and he'd just begun to hope that his past might not catch up with him.

The police came and banged on our front door and Sadiq was almost wetting himself. He couldn't work out whether to lock himself in the bathroom or hide in a wardrobe. But it turned out the police and Georgie's dad weren't there to see Sadiq. What they wanted was a word with our sister.

By the time Sadiq had composed himself enough to tell the police he didn't recognise their authority, and to denounce George Smith as a little Hitler who wasn't welcome in our home, Fatima had got Melissa making everyone a cup of tea.

The police were all crammed into our front room on the rickety chairs and the beaten-up old sofa. George Smith was perched on one of the arms looking world-weary. Even so, he was smiling as though he couldn't quite believe he was sitting down for a cuppa with a bunch of British Bangladeshis.

"Sadiq, shut up please and help Melissa in the kitchen," said Fatima. To my surprise, Sadiq did exactly what he was told.

For a while it was like no one could remember exactly why they were there. The big clock on the wall ticked loudly. People coughed and cleared their throats as if they were about to speak. My sister, who had this strange look on her face, didn't seem to want to help the situation. I kept hoping my parents would return. But they were probably browsing in one of the pound shops where my father loved to look for bargains.

Finally, George Smith began talking in that rasping voice I remembered from Cable Street. It had this dangerous edge to it, like some of the voices you hear when you walk past pubs late at night.

"So, Fatima, we meet again."

He seemed to find this funny and his famous blue eyes sparkled.

"Sounds like a line from a film or something," he said. "Like I'm Batman and you're Cat Woman."

Fatima touched her fingertips together.

"You wouldn't be Batman, Mr Smith. He's one of the good guys."

"Touché, Fatima," he chuckled. "Well, we may have to agree to differ on who the good guys are. The thing is, I'm here to ask for your help."

He swivelled round to face one of the police officers.

"That's how I want to keep this. Just a friendly chat, not an interrogation or anything."

"You shouldn't really say anything until her parents get back," the policeman muttered.

Fatima shook her head slowly.

"I'm not your friend, Mr Smith, but I am a friend of Georgie's. If helping you doesn't hurt him, I'm prepared to listen."

Smith rubbed the dark stubble on his chin with the palm of his hand. In the silent room it sounded like he'd taken a sheet of sandpaper to his whiskers.

"Have you seen Georgie since that day in Cable Street?"

The three policemen and the policewoman all shuffled awkwardly in their seats. It was clear to them that my sister was blind and couldn't *see* anyone or anything.

"I'm sorry, darling. I mean, I know you've spoken to him, but have you actually met up with him?"

Fatima laughed in that way that always reminded me of tinkling wind chimes.

"I don't need to see Georgie to know he's all right, Mr Smith. I speak to him, yes, although he doesn't really want to talk to anyone at the moment. He feels confused. He still believes he did the right thing when he crossed from your side to ours, but he doubts you'll ever understand."

Smith scratched at the bristles on his right cheek.

"Look, Fatima, shall we cut to the chase? I want Georgie back home with me. So do my wife and daughter. We're all frantic with worry, to be honest with you. I know London's a big place, but I can't believe it's so difficult to track down a young boy."

He flashed a look of annoyance at the police officers.

"I also don't understand why there were possible sightings of him the first couple of weeks he was away, but they've all stopped now. The police reckon he's not sleeping out on the streets any more. They think someone's helping him stay hidden – that he's in a squat, maybe, or even someone's house."

He broke off suddenly and looked up at the ceiling. His head was cocked on one side like a dog straining to hear telltale sounds from upstairs.

"He's not here with you, is he?"

Fatima smiled serenely.

"I can't tell you where he is. I just know he's safe."

Smith struck the side of the sofa with a fist.

"I'm getting the hump with you now, Fatima. Do you mean you can't tell me where he is, or you won't?"

The dark-haired policewoman took hold of Smith's coat sleeve as though she feared he might leap up and hit my sister.

"Mr Smith, I am happy to cooperate with

you and the police. I sense how upset you are, but the only way you'll get your son home is if he wants to go back himself. Force won't work. It didn't work in Cable Street and it won't now."

At that moment, Melissa appeared in the doorway with a tray full of my mother's best china cups and saucers. She looked shocked. George Smith, with his politician's instincts, seemed to sense it was time to change his line of attack.

"Hello, young lady," he said, all charming again. "I believe I've also had the pleasure of meeting you before, haven't I?"

Melissa started to shrug and the cups slid from one side of the tray to the other as though we were on a ship at sea.

"It's a simple question I'd like to ask you. Do you know where my son is?"

He had got to his feet and was reaching to take the tray from Melissa's uncertain grasp.

Fatima raised her hand.

"You don't have to answer him, Melissa.

You don't have to talk to him at all if you don't want to."

Melissa was starring wide-eyed at Smith. I wondered if she was having some kind of Cable Street flashback. Then her mouth began to work like a fish struggling to breathe.

"I did just speak to him when I was in the kitchen, as it goes," she said finally.

Smith nodded. The bald policeman with the purple veins in his nose leant forward in his chair.

"If you'd just like to hand over your mobile, we can probably use it to track him down," he said gruffly.

Melissa swayed from side to side like a big tree in a forest about to fall.

"It wasn't on a mobile. It doesn't work like that. He seemed really scared, I mean, he was terrified. He said there's someone after him who wants to hurt him. He said their name was Jack."

HYUN-MI

Night in the nearest big Chinese town to the border is scary, but exciting too. The neon lights and garish advertising hoardings make the whole place look like a giant fairground. In North Korea there is no advertising, just posters of the Dear Leader. State-run stores are where you're supposed to do your shopping – drab, grey buildings that don't bother to let you know they're there.

In China, if you have money, you can buy McDonald's and Coca Cola; the glitzy adverts make them look like the food and drink of the gods. I've never seen such things before.

In North Korea there are no fast food restaurants. At times in North Korea there is no food, full stop.

During the famines and food shortages in my country, people boil up grass to make soup. Imagine that! You see them squatting by the side of the road, collecting it in bags. Sometimes, as I drove by with my father in his limousine, I'd see them keel over with hunger. Sometimes they'd force clumps of it into their mouths but it would stick in their parched throats.

One journey with my father still haunts me. It replays in my mind like a film.

I am sitting up front in his shiny black limo.

"How can they eat plain grass?" I ask him as he swerves around the potholes in the badly rutted road. "Surely it's no good for humans."

I look across at him in the driver's seat and I wonder if there are tears in his eyes.

"It shouldn't be like this," he says. "The Americans have sent proper food for the people to eat. But the Dear Leader is keeping it just for the army and his friends."

"We are his friends, though, aren't we?" I ask.

"Yes, dearest one, but not by choice. I hope that one day you may have the chance to see other places in the world and discover the truth about our homeland. In other countries there is plenty for everyone to eat. People are treated with dignity there."

"Why don't you take me, Papa? It would be fun to travel with you."

He tries to smile.

"Because we can never leave. Not together, anyway. I don't think the Dear Leader will invite me to travel with him again when he next goes to China or Russia. He's not so happy with me these days. And for you, a female, there is no possibility of escape. . ."

Suddenly I scream, "Papa stop!" and instinctively his foot slams down on the brake pedal.

A frail old woman, more ancient than my grandmother, has wandered into the road. My father has managed to stop the car just a foot or so away from her. The old woman stands there swaying, as if in a breeze, staring at us through the dusty windscreen. Then, without making a sound, she closes her eyes and falls forward onto the bonnet. Her face is still angled towards me. It is more skull than skin.

I scream again and again. It is the only sound apart from the low noise of the car engine. Then it occurs to me that my father hasn't switched it off. He is still sitting there with his seatbelt on. He hasn't got out of the car. I know we haven't hit the old woman; she has collapsed because she is weak with hunger. Why won't my father help her?

I stare at him now. He is breathing heavily and drops of sweat are falling from his forehead. Finally, he reaches down and puts the limo into reverse. I gasp as we begin to inch backwards. Whatever is he doing? Slowly the old woman slides off the bonnet and disappears from our view. It is like watching one of my china dolls fall down the side of my bed.

We back up a few more feet until we can

see her crumpled form just lying there. I want
to shout at my father, to demand that he take
care of her. But it seems his mind is made up.
He turns the steering wheel and manoeuvres
around the bundle of bones and rags just as if he
was making his way around a hole in the road.
Then he puts his foot down on the accelerator
and we speed away.

Neither of us speaks for a long time.

"Was she dead?" I ask finally.

"I don't know," my father whispers.

"You're a doctor, Papa. You're supposed to
help people."

"That is true, dearest one. But there was
nothing I could do for her. There is nothing
I can do for any of our people."

★★★

I shiver and pull my blanket around me. I am
in China now and that hot, distant day is long
gone. So is the old woman and so is my father.
I have taken my chance to run from North Korea

but China, my new home, is no paradise.

I am hiding in a construction site, on the upper floor of an unfinished office block. It is just the skeleton of a building; there is no roof to stop the rain pouring in. Security guards patrol the site at night, shining their torches everywhere, tripping over building equipment and swearing loudly. If they discover you, they kick you awake and yell at you until you run down the half-made stairs and away. But my biggest fear is the Chinese police. If they catch me, I will be deported back to North Korea and a prison camp.

It's hard to sleep, but when I do, I often dream of that old woman in the dusty North Korean road. Then I wonder if my father's actions that day made him a bad person. The thought nags at me like toothache but in the end I reject it. My father was a good man, a sane man in a mad world. He was nothing like the Dear Leader and his cronies.

I talk to Fatima often. She can't speak Korean, of course, but when you communicate by telepathy it doesn't have to be in actual words.

Often it's like your thoughts and memories and emotions just flow out of you and merge with the other person's. Then they can understand everything you think and feel. It's hard to explain if you've never done it. But the truth is, if Fatima hadn't found me and tuned in to my deepest needs and fears, I don't think I could have made it.

Try and rest, she tells me. *I am sending someone to you. I promise they'll be there soon.*

Even though I am lying on a cold, concrete floor in a dangerous foreign land, that thought makes me smile.

MELISSA

At school, Leona, Kodi and Simone could talk about nothing but the *Celebrity Skin* TV show and last night's 'Underwear Challenge'. All the has-been soap stars, pop singers and dancers were running out of clothes now, because every time they lost a challenge they had to remove something. The show had been on for a few weeks and it was obvious we would soon be seeing the first celebrity to strip down to their birthday suit. Not that any of the contestants seemed to mind all that much - most of them seemed desperate to show off their bodies to the world 24/7.

"The radiators in that *Celebrity Skin* house must be turned right up cos it's freezing outside. No way would I walk round in the buff in this weather," Kodi said.

Leona pouted thoughtfully.

"Yeah, but if you could win a hundred thousand pounds..."

Artsem laughed behind his tiny hand and rocked back on his chair.

"Man, it's disgusting. Even if you win the whole thing, everyone gets to see you in your underpants. No way would I go on that programme."

"No way would anyone ask you, Artsem," Leona said.

"Innit, though," chorused Kodi and Simone.

I had to admit that I'd been watching *Celebrity Skin* just like the rest of the class, but even I could see it was what Miss de Souza, our teacher, called "exploitative of everyone involved, including the audience".

"It is trash, though," I said. "It makes me feel bad for watching it."

Leona turned round slowly to inspect me.

"But Melissa, now that you're a celebrity, what with you being on the news and everything, maybe you could be on *Celebrity Skin*."

I sensed that Artsem and Mikhail were about to say something so I flashed them my *Don't even think about it* look. They said nothing.

"My friend Fatima says it's degrading. She says it's a shame that television can't be used for more important things."

I could see them all frowning at me.

"I don't mean instead of stuff like *Celebrity Skin*, I mean as well as."

Kodi curled her lip.

"You mean like educational things. There's all those nature programmes. You could always watch something about hippos, Melissa, if you don't want to see celebrities getting naked."

"Kodi, yeah, be careful talking about me and hippos in the same sentence. I wouldn't want you to get hurt, understand?"

Kodi blushed.

"No, Melissa, I didn't mean nothing about your weight. Really. I was just saying, you know. . ."

I ignored her.

"Since Cable Street when we stopped the Fascists from marching, I've been a bit more interested in what's going on in the world," I said. "Maybe there should be things on TV about politics and stuff for kids."

Artsem snorted again.

"No one would watch that when they can see some guy getting whacked by a giant cotton bud and knocked into a pool of gunge."

And then my hero Kele spoke.

"I might watch a programme about politics. In fact, I did. I saw this thing called *Question Time* the other night. It was all right, as it goes."

Leona started purring. Ever since she'd seen Kele on the TV she was all over him.

"Kel, that clip of you at Cable Street after you stopped the Fascists. Innit, you can see it on YouTube now?"

Kele gave her this big goofy grin.

"Yeah, I seen it, Leona. I reckon that TV crew got my best side!"

He pulled this stupid face like he was an actor posing for a photo. Don't get me wrong, I loved Kele in many ways, but sometimes he made me sick.

GeoRGie

The burnt-out flat I'd been hiding in was on the edge of the estate where Melissa lived with her mum. There were twenty blocks, each six storeys high, all huddled around sunless squares of cracked concrete. Walkways ran along each floor, linking the flats. Some were boarded up with signs in red paint saying 'Keep Out'. From above, the estate must have looked like a prison.

For three days and nights I'd kept away. When Fatima warned me that my dad and the police were coming, I grabbed my things and ran. But back on the streets I felt exposed.

Jack could be anywhere, closing in on me, watching me as I bedded down for the night.

I climbed the steps of the block where Melissa had found a hiding place for me. The stench of urine in the stairwell made my nostrils flare. It was almost dark. The wall lights, which were protected by small wire cages, were either flickering or dead. I passed the third floor, the fourth floor.

The stairwell came out in the middle of the topmost walkway. I looked over the edge and gulped. I'd forgotten how high up it was. To my right was the boarded-up flat that had been my hideaway, fire damaged and damp. I tapped on the plywood nailed across the door. Nothing. Then I saw a shape move behind a frosted glass window to one side where the boards had been removed.

Melissa, is that you?

I forced the window open and hoisted myself up so my chest was balanced on the narrow sill. Then, palms stretched out in front of me, I slithered down onto the scorched black floorboards and strips of charred carpet below.

"Welcome home," a voice said from the shadows. "I reckon you could stay here forever now. The police don't believe you was even here at all. And the Council will never get round to doing it up again."

Melissa had brought two shopping bags of supplies for me. Without even thanking her, I tore the wrapper off a meat pie and began to devour it.

"You eat like a pig, Georgie."

"You're the best, Melissa," I said between mouthfuls.

"I know. That's what everyone says."

The flat was freezing. We could see our breath as we spoke.

"So what did the police say?"

"They was really angry. They said we'd wasted their time. Fatima told them straight up about telepathy and how we speak to you and that made them even madder. I think your dad believed us, though. He knows, Georgie, doesn't he?"

"Yeah, he knows. I've told him, anyway."

"Don't you want to talk things over with him? I never even met my dad. I know yours is a Fascist and everything but don't you think you should see if he's changed? We're all different since Cable Street. Maybe he is too."

"He'd have to have changed a lot. He'd have to accept that I've got friends like you, for a start."

Melissa gave this little girly smile.

"That's a nice thing to say, Georgie."

"I'm serious."

She watched me wipe my mouth with the back of my hand.

"What did you think of the pie?"

"Awesome. The best pie ever."

"I'd better be going. My mum's noticed me jacking things from the fridge. I don't want to give you away again."

I glanced at the window. Melissa had never come into the flat before. I couldn't see how she could possibly have squeezed her body through the narrow opening, or how she was going to leave.

"Remember I can read your mind," she said, one eyebrow raised. "And if you'd bothered to read mine you'd know that the front door is unlocked."

She opened it and, without looking back, headed off along the walkway into the night.

★★★

I woke with the smell of smoke in my nostrils, having dreamt I was leaning by the cooker at home chatting with my mum. But it wasn't the smell of Sunday custard bubbling over onto the electric rings, it was the sour whiff of my burnt-out hideaway.

The wind was whistling through a broken pane of glass above my head and I could hear hail spattering like shotgun pellets against those windows that were still in one piece. I'd fallen asleep in the dark but it was getting light now.

I looked up at the soot grimed ceiling, then over at the wall above the lifeless radiator.

I shuddered and started to scream. In blood red paint, someone had written me a message:

GEORGIE MUST DIE.

HYUN-MI

The day the police came for my father, I knew something was wrong. When I got home from school he threw his arms around me and held me tightly against his chest. He was pale and whiskery – my father never went a day without shaving! He was not a drinker but I smelled alcohol on his breath.

"It's over, dearest one. I have been reported to the authorities. One of the doctors at the hospital heard me cursing the Dear Leader under my breath. That's a crime that can never be forgiven. I'm afraid I have ruined us all."

I freed myself from his grasp.

"Then you must apologise to the Dear Leader, Papa. Say it was all a misunderstanding. Surely he will listen to you."

He placed both his hands on my shoulders and stared into my eyes. What he said next sounded like madness but I had no doubt he was serious.

"If you are to have any chance, Hyun-mi, you must run. They will come for you, and your grandmother as well. It is the cruel way of our country that whole families are sent to the prison camps if even one of them does something wrong."

"But where will I go?"

Tears were spilling down his cheeks now.

"I don't know. You must hide amongst the street orphans. There are thousands of them - many have lost their parents in the famines. Compared to theirs, your life has been very comfortable, but you must become hard, Hyun-mi. That way you may yet live."

"I would rather come with you and Grandmother to prison."

He wiped his eyes. Suddenly he was very business-like and I heard the tone he used with his hospital staff.

"In prison, Hyun-mi, none of us would survive, that much is certain. I know that if you run you will probably die on the streets. But prove me wrong, dearest one. Find a way to live on, for me. Please prove me wrong!"

I heard the sound of boots tramping up the stairs to our apartment. Fear flashed across my father's face.

"Go into the kitchen and climb out onto the window ledge. Wait there until they have taken us."

I tried to hug him but he shoved me away.

"Mother, they are here," he cried, and I saw my grandmother's tiny, birdlike face appear at her bedroom door.

"Go now, Hyun-mi, and save yourself!" she said.

They didn't bother to knock. The door to our apartment splintered as they kicked it in. My father tried to talk down to them, to show them he was still a man of importance, but they ignored him. I could hear shouting as the policemen ripped through the flat, tearing open wardrobes and cupboards. They ransacked the kitchen, too, but they didn't look out onto the ledge where I was hiding.

"Where is your daughter? We were told that three of you lived here."

My father's voice was raised too now. The walls of our building were thin and I could hear every word.

"She is staying with a school friend. It's just my mother and myself."

"You lie!" one of the policeman screamed back at him. He must have knocked my father down because I heard the crash of falling furniture and shattering glass. I also heard my grandmother wail.

"How dare you! We are loyal subjects of the Dear Leader and his father, the Great Leader, before him. My son is the Dear Leader's personal physician. This is an outrage!"

They must have struck my poor grandmother

too. She gave a little cry and then was silent.

On the ledge outside our apartment, I covered my mouth with my hand. I was sobbing and shivering but I knew they must not hear me. I inched along so the policemen would not see me unless they leant right outside. The walls of our building had been damaged by years of wintry weather. I clung on with aching fingers to a deep crack that ran from the top of the kitchen window to the apartment above.

Far below me the Taedong River snaked through our capital city. I could see the Arch of Triumph – at school they told us it was taller than the one in a country called France. To the left was the fifty-storey luxury hotel that my father said was always empty.

My father and his big mouth. Look where it had got us. My poor, darling father. I knew he would rather die than give me away to the police.

I must have stayed outside for half an hour, clinging like a frozen climber to the side of a mountain. All the time, I was crying as quietly as I could. Finally, I watched the police leave. They bundled my grandmother's crumpled body into their van then threw my father in after her. I knew I would never see them again. The thought seemed to suck all the air from my lungs.

I was utterly alone and terrified about the future, but it seemed that my instinct to survive was strong. Even as the police van was driving away, I promised myself that I would toughen up. I would escape from the capital and find a way to flee from North Korea. I was not going to die. I was going to prove my dear father wrong.

FATIMA

When you're blind, you don't worry about the little details of life. It makes me cringe sometimes the way people get so hung up about stuff, especially their appearance. I don't even know what I look like! People tell me I'm pretty, though maybe they're just being kind. Whatever. I suppose my blindness makes it easier for me to focus on the important things – like what's on the inside.

Something else people tell me is that I'm brave. The newspapers and the TV called us heroes for standing up to George Smith and his fascist thugs. To me it was just about doing the right thing. He wanted to terrorise the Muslim people who live around Cable Street and someone had to stop him.

That's another thing I need to put straight. I didn't just stand up for those people because I'm a Muslim too. It wouldn't have mattered to me whether they were Hindus, Christians or whatever. George Smith was behaving like a bully and you have to stand up to bullies.

Which brings me to Jack. I knew that Georgie, Melissa and Omar would have freaked out if I'd told them what I had planned. But it just seemed the obvious thing to do. This Jack was tormenting my friend. He'd scared my little brother. I didn't like that.

Jack had claimed to have a special interest in me, so I decided to reach out to him. I let him know that I was prepared for the two of us to meet, any time, anywhere. Like I say, Georgie, Melissa and Omar would have gone crazy if they'd known.

I suppose I expected him to contact me in advance, but that's not how it happened. For once everyone had gone out. My father was at the restaurant, Sadiq was with his university friends, Omar had gone to take some food to Georgie, my mother was round at my aunt's place. When we were all there the house seemed so cramped and noisy. Sometimes I liked being at home on my own.

I don't know how he got inside, but we were not really very security conscious. My mother used to moan at my father because he kept a front door key on a string that you could pull through the letterbox. "Who would want to break in here?" my father would say to her. "We've got nothing worth stealing."

I was in my bedroom when I heard someone moving downstairs. I assumed it was Omar. I was keen to hear from him how Georgie was coping. I stepped out onto the landing and called down the stairs.

"How is he, Omar? Did you take him that medicine for his cough?"

Silence. My family don't play games with me. It's not exactly cool to sneak up on someone who's blind and shout, "Boo!"

Was it a burglar? I felt my legs go wobbly.

"You can take whatever you find, but we've got nothing, really. Have the telly if you can carry it!"

Then I heard him.

My name is Jack. I know that you can hear me. Please be afraid. . .!

I felt my way back into my bedroom and sat down on my bed. His footsteps sounded slowly up the stairs.

"Come on, Fatima, you said this is what you wanted," I told myself as I fidgeted with the tassels on my bedspread.

He was standing just outside my door. I could hear him breathing.

So, you're the famous girl who defeated the Fascists. I'm very pleased to meet you.

"Why don't you talk normally to me?" I said.

I prefer to use my thought-voice.

"It's a gift. You should use it for good. Not to frighten people."

I heard the floorboards creak as he shuffled from one foot to the other. I waited for him to say something but he didn't reply.

"I've touched a nerve, haven't I? Why do you use your gift to terrorise people when you could do so much good with it?"

Silence again.

"I bet it's because you've been hurt. Someone's rejected you — a partner, your family maybe. You're behaving this way because you're mad at the world."

That's when he slapped me round the side of the head and sent me tumbling to the floor.

I lay there for a few seconds wondering if he would attack me again. I hadn't felt this angry since Cable Street.

HOW DARE YOU? HOW DARE YOU STRIKE ME?

Georgie told me that when he first heard my thought-voice it was like a nuclear bomb going off inside his head. When I'm desperate to talk to someone, or they're trying to block me out, I do the equivalent of screaming at the top of my lungs. Then they feel intense pain.

This Jack, whoever he was, began to scream. At the time I didn't think about it, but he sounded less like a grown man than a teenager. He fell heavily against the door frame, then collapsed onto the landing floor.

I sent a whole ocean of thought-waves crashing over him.

HOW DARE YOU BREAK INTO MY HOUSE? HOW DARE YOU THREATEN ME?

I heard him stagger down the staircase, bouncing off the walls. He wrenched open the front door than pulled it shut behind him.

Of course, I felt relieved that I'd driven him away, but then I wondered if I'd been reckless. I wasn't really sure what effect I'd had on him. Once I'd managed to knock Georgie unconscious by mind-screaming at him. What if Jack stumbled into the road and fell under a bus? I know Melissa thinks I'm soppy sometimes, but I felt I should try to make things better.

I called after him. It was a soothing voice now.

*It's Fatima. I know that you can hear me.
Please don't be afraid.*

For a moment there was silence, then, faintly
at first, I found his thought-waves rippling back
to me.

Leave me alone. Please just leave me.

Soon, I'd located him. I was inside his head
and what I found there made me gasp. He was
not some bogeyman. This creature who'd been
threatening Omar, Georgie and now me, was
not an adult at all. He was just a boy.

*Why do you want to hurt us, Jack? It seems to me
you're only hurting yourself.*

His troubled mind was whimpering now.

*I just want to be left alone. I keep hearing you
all reaching out to me. I don't want to part of anything.
I just want you to leave me be.*

Not to sound big-headed, but sometimes
I think I understand what's really on people's
minds quicker than they do themselves.

*Jack, I don't believe you do want to be left alone.
Wasn't it you who contacted us? You're pushing
me away with one hand. But with the other*

you're reaching out for our help.

Again there was silence.

Think it over, Jack. We have the same gift as you, but we want to use it wisely. Join us, Jack. It's never too late to change.

Melissa says I'm too good to be true sometimes – she calls me 'Little Miss Perfect'. But I was being sincere with Jack. I wanted him to know that I meant every word I said.

JACK

You have to understand, I hate happy families. I get angry just seeing them walk down the street. I'm there shivering with a blanket wrapped around me, and some cute little five-year-old with golden curls squeals, "Mummy, Daddy, what's wrong with that boy? Why is he sitting there like that? Why is he so dirty?"

Then the parents get embarrassed. They hold on to their little angel extra tight. Maybe the mum, who's all made-up and rich-looking, starts to blush and stammer, "Just keep walking, darling. I'll explain later."

Then off they go, hand in hand. I wonder

what they say *later* when they're back in their safe, warm houses with the cream-coloured carpets and cupboards crammed with food.

"It's all very sad, darling, but you see, he hasn't got a nice home and parents who love him."

Maybe they just change the subject and forget I even exist. Like I say, I hate happy families.

It's the dads I glare at most when they pass by. I know why they get to me. I talked about it with Mrs Ali, my counsellor. That's when I was still at home in Leeds and going to secondary school. She said I had to come to terms with the fact that my own dad, who walked out, wasn't perfect, and neither was my step-father. Most of what Mrs Ali said was rubbish, but she was spot on about that. My dads were "not the best role models".

What they did teach me was how to use my fists. Both of them were handy like that. To be fair to my real dad, it was mostly just slaps and smacks I got from him. But Davey, my step-dad, used to punch me when he got mad. This ugly, squashed nose of mine is all thanks to Davey.

Every time I see my reflection in a shop or restaurant window, I think of him.

So where was my mum? Why didn't she step in? Well, it turned out she loved Davey more than me. I told her straight, "If he ever touches me again, I'm off."

She replied, "Don't make me choose between you, Jackie. You're my baby, but he's my fella and I need him."

Of course, Davey paid for her hair and her holidays and her drinks till she fell off her barstool every night. How could I compete with that?

Next time he hit me, I left.

It was when I reached London that I started hearing voices – lots of them. I thought I was going bonkers. It was like my head was a scanner and it was tuning in to all these different radio stations. These kids – and they were all kids – sounded like they belonged to the biggest, happiest family of all time. But I didn't need anybody. I wanted to be left alone.

At night, when I was trying to get to sleep

under a railway arch or in a subway, I'd hear them chattering, joking, sharing, comforting. I didn't want to listen in, but I couldn't help it. Their happy babble drove me crazy. One name kept coming up in their conversations: Fatima. She was the one I grew to hate the most.

In the end, I decided to get back at them. I'd find out where they were going and follow them around. Frighten them. Maybe even hurt them.

Fatima and her brother Omar lived in Whitechapel, in the East End of London. I'd heard of Whitechapel. My step-dad was obsessed with true crime books and the ones he read the most were about Jack the Ripper, the Victorian serial killer.

It gave me an idea. I'd talk to them after all, but I wouldn't be Jack, the real me. I'd be Jack the Ripper, returned from the dead. See how they liked that!

And it worked. It was a brilliant trick - like impersonating another person's voice. I created this character in my mind - a bogeyman, a murderer. When I used telepathy with Fatima and Omar and their special friend Georgie, I could make myself be him.

My name is Jack. I know that you can hear me. Please be afraid!

But it turns out I was only fooling myself. Fatima saw through my act. She understood just how lonely I was. I'd never known anyone like her. I wanted to be her friend.

GEORGIE

I was hungry, but for once, thanks to Omar, I had money in my pocket. The windows of the first café I came to were clouded by condensation so I couldn't see in. I eased open the door which seemed to have warped in its frame.

Inside it was like the engine room of an old steamship – cutlery clanged and everyone seemed to be talking at once. I found an empty table in a corner and sat down to look at the grease-stained menu.

Behind the counter, wrestling with a large machine that seemed to be pumping out tea, coffee and smoke, was a grouchy looking man with dark, slicked back hair.

"All right, all right," he shouted at some workmen who were moaning that he'd not produced their orders.

Next to my table sat an old woman. Her face looked crinkled and yellow like a book that's been left out in the sun. She was murmuring softly to herself. In front of her was a cup of tea she'd barely touched.

"Kid, you can't sit there. You'll have to go."

It was the owner. He pushed his greasy hair back from his face then gestured with a thumb towards the door.

"I just want some beans on toast," I said. "I've got the money. I'll give it to you up front if you like."

"Take a look at yourself, kid. You're no good for business."

I glanced down at my hands. They were filthy with dirt.

"Just go," he said. "And don't come back."

The old lady stirred back to life. For a second I thought she might defend me.

"Oi, Melv!" she called to the owner.

"What?"

"It's disgusting, innit? The state of kids today."

I slammed the door behind me.

I'd walked a hundred yards when I saw two boys of about sixteen. Both were skinheads with green bomber jackets and number one crops - a style I'd seen a lot at my dad's political meetings. Despite their matching close-shaved hair, physically they were very different.

A fat skin and a skinny skin, I thought.

I knew to keep my head down and walk past them - no eye contact. But as I got closer they stopped and blocked my way.

"You got a light, mate?" the fat one asked.

Both skins had badges pinned to their jackets, the red and white cross of St George, and various symbols and abbreviations I half recognised.

"I said, have you got a light?"

I looked into his close-set piggy eyes.

"Sorry, I don't smoke."

He moved to let me pass, then grabbed me by the shoulder.

"Wait a minute. I know you."

"I don't think so," I muttered.

"Yeah, I do. I've seen you at the British Fascist Party rallies. I never forget a face."

His skinny mate started laughing this weird laugh.

"I'll tell you who that is, Del. He's Georgie Smith.

I could feel the electricity coming off them now.

"You're a traitor, that's what you are - a disgrace to your race. And so's your old man. I seen him on the TV the other night saying he's giving up on politics."

"I haven't seen him in weeks," I said.

My words were thick and sticky in my mouth. I could feel a muscle twitching madly in my jaw.

"What's happened to you, anyway?" the skinny skin said. "You look like a tramp."

I ignored him.

"Oi, if I ask you a question, I expect an answer."

He pushed me hard in the chest and I took a step backwards.

"How come you look like a dosser?"

I expected him to hit me, but suddenly he dropped his hands. A thick-set figure had crossed the street and was now standing alongside me. He was no older than the skinheads but he was built like a boxer. His nose had been broken so badly it had almost turned round on itself. When he spoke, he snuffled like a Boxer dog.

"What's the problem?"

The skinny skin narrowed his eyes.

"It's nothing to do with you, mate. We're just having a friendly chat."

"Doesn't look friendly to me."

The fat skin rolled his shoulders and his neck as though he was limbering up for something.

"It's none of your business, mate. Just leave us to it, will you?"

"I'm making it my business," the boy said.

The skinheads flashed a look at each other.

"Do you know who this is?" the skinny skin asked, pointing at me.

"Yeah, I know," the boy grunted. "He's Georgie Smith."

I swung around to look at him properly.

"Then you know he's a scumbag and a traitor to his race," the fat skin said.

"Look, just run along and play, will you?" the boy said. "If you try and fight me you'll both get hurt."

"Is that right?"

The fat skin curled his lip and raised his fists.

"Come on then!"

He didn't even see the Boxer boy's right hook. It landed *smack* on his fleshy chin. The fat skin collapsed as if he'd been punctured, then lay gurgling on the pavement.

The other skinhead took a moment to respond. He jumped on top of the boy and punched him twice in the side of his face.

The boy barely flinched. He soon had the skinny skin's arms wrapped up, then he lifted him up onto his back as though he weighed no more than his bomber jacket. The skinhead thrashed and squirmed as they lurched towards a pile of black bin bags by the side of the road. With a drop of his shoulder, the boy threw the skinhead on top of them.

The skinny skin was coughing and shouting curses but he didn't seem to want to fight any more.

The next thing I heard was the screech of tyres as a white police van pulled up on the pavement next to us. The driver jumped out.

"What the hell's going on?" he shouted.

The fat skinhead was back on his feet now, rubbing his grazed chin. "That kid's a nutter! He just attacked us for no reason."

The skinny skin was keeping his distance but he called out too.

"He should be locked up. He's mental."

The policeman turned to inspect the boy. "Well?"

He just nodded in my direction.

"They were out of order, officer. They were picking on my friend here."

"Is that a fact?"

The policeman looked at the two skins and raised an eyebrow.

"Anyway, you can all go home now. Whatever's happened here is over. Understand?"

The two skins waited until the policeman was back in his van and the boy and I had gone maybe fifty yards up the road. Then they started calling after us. Well, me, really. I was a disgrace to my race because I had friends who weren't white. I was a traitor to the British Fascist Party because I'd swapped sides.

The boy gave me this strange look.

"And you used to hang out with people like that?"

I laughed.

"It feels like a long time ago now. People change."

I offered him my hand to shake.

"I owe you big time."

"That's OK," he said. "I'm a runaway too. I know the kind of scrapes you can get into. The truth is, it's me who owes you."

I shrugged. What was he talking about?

"My name's Jack," he said. "And I've got some explaining to do."

I did a double take.

"Jack?"

"I'm afraid so."

"The 'Jack' who's been following me?"

He nodded.

"But your thought-voice. You sound like an adult – a really scary one."

He grimaced.

"It's just a trick. I sort of created this character in my mind. When I use telepathy I can make myself be him."

I admit I totally lost it. I was screaming curses at him and swinging my fists. He didn't even put his hands up to protect himself. I'm no fighter, but I know I hurt him. The flesh around his left eye started to swell like an overripe piece of fruit, then a trickle of blood leaked out of his battered nose. I was panting and wheezing and swearing and hitting.

And he just took it.

HYUN-MI

I am in a smart hotel in the Chinese border town where I arrived, half-drowned, a fortnight ago. I have begged for money on the street outside this very building. Now, I am sitting in the reception area on a leather sofa.

The business travellers checking in stare at me. That's because I can't stop smiling. I am wearing new clothes given to me by some charity workers who help North Korean refugees. I have just met a young woman I know only as Sun. She is making arrangements for me to travel from China to a new life in South Korea.

I have heard so much propaganda about our 'bitter enemies' from the South. The two Koreas were once one country. But war has left us split down the middle. The border between North and South is the most heavily guarded in the world with hundreds of thousands of soldiers massed on both sides. No one can cross it, which is why North Koreans try to escape through China.

Sun should be my enemy then, but, of course, she does not seem like one and, compared to North Korea, the South sounds like heaven.

Perhaps it's her name that makes me want to like her. It reminds me of Sun-joo, my dearest North Korean friend.

I met Sun-joo a week after my father and grandmother were taken away. She was a street child living in a town two days' walk from Pyongyang.

I was sheltering in a deserted railway station when she found me. Outside, snowflakes were falling, fluttering from the night sky like clouds of white moths. I'd curled up on a wooden bench and, though it seemed impossible to sleep when I was so cold and hungry, I must have dozed off.

"Do you want that newspaper?"

I woke to find the round face of a teenage girl peering down at me. She was pointing at a rolled up paper further along the bench.

"I can't read that well, but I like to tear out all the pictures of the Dear Leader. Some of them I just rip to shreds there and then!"

I started to smile but stopped myself. Maybe this was a trick, to test my loyalty.

"Did you know, they arrested an old man at this very station for sitting on a newspaper that carried a photo of Kim Jong-il? The old man said it was an accident – said he'd never sit on the Dear Leader deliberately. But the police would have none of it. They marched him off to a prison camp and. . ."

She mimed a noose being tightened around the old man's neck.

"You don't believe it?"

"I do," I stammered.

"Doesn't matter what you think. It's true –

or something like it is. Of course, I would definitely be strung up if they knew what I do with certain of the Kim Jong-il pictures in my collection."

She waited for me to respond. I just shrugged.

"Toilet paper!" she squealed. "That's all the Dear Leader is good for!"

I laughed too. I'd never met anyone like her. She became serious.

"You don't look like a street kid. I can see from your hands you've never done any work. You haven't had to scrabble in the mud for bits of grain that the farmers drop or beg for scraps from the army. What's your name, princess?"

"Hyun-mi."

"I'm Sun-joo. That's what my parents called me. They're gone now – thanks to our Comrade Kim Jong-il."

She started to whistle the tune of *No Motherland Without You*.

"Do you know what? My own mother

hated that song. And thinking about her makes me feel all sentimental."

She narrowed her eyes and looked me up and down.

"If you like, I could be a bit of a mother to you, Hyun-mi. I'll look after you, teach you how to survive on the streets. It's a once in a lifetime offer. If you say no, I guarantee you'll end up dead."

What could I say? I nodded.

"Thank you, Sun-joo."

"Precious as a jewel, according to my name. To be honest, it would be a better name for you, princess. It doesn't really work for me."

★★★

I'm sitting now in a plush hotel with a South Korean woman called Sun. She is going to rescue me from a beggar's life in China. But it's thanks to Sun-joo, my North Korean friend, that I'm alive at all.

She taught me how to steal rice from the

market without having my ear twisted off by a farmer's wife, or getting smashed in the ribs by some club-wielding peasant. She knew how to cheek the soldiers into throwing her a bone they'd finished gnawing on. And then she'd share it with me. Sun-joo was more precious to me than any jewel.

She seemed to know all the street kids we came across but I was the only one she was close to. And she cared for me as well as any mother. When I told her one day that I'd heard the voice of Fatima, a faraway girl, telling me to head for the border with China, Sun-joo didn't laugh.

"Then it's to the Chinese border we must go, princess."

We walked at night along empty highways, caught a lift on a slow-moving train, then jumped off into thorny bushes when we were spotted by a guard. I was covered in scratches and so was Sun-joo, but nothing was broken. We lay there giggling.

"You see those stars?" I said as the train chugged away into the distance. "People in free countries can see them too."

She lifted herself up on one elbow.

"You deserve to be free, princess. You shouldn't have to live like this."

Finally we reached the hills near the border town of Musan. The memory of that day will live with me forever - it plays in my head, again and again. I see Sun-joo and me together as though I am outside myself.

We are high up on a hillside looking down into the valley. Below us is the Tumen River. It does not shimmer under the cloudy sky. It just rolls along, flat and brown.

I squeeze Sun-joo's hand.

"Doesn't look too difficult to cross," I say.

Then I spy the border guards patrolling with their guns. We are up so high they look like tiny green birds.

I am still feeling confident. The river stretches for miles in both directions. The guards cannot be everywhere and at night we can surely slip past them.

Sun-joo stares down into the valley.

Her forehead is creased by a frown.

"So that's the point where we have to swim for it?" she says.

"Only a little way. It's not that wide."

"And on the other side we'll be free and we can eat all day and dance all night."

"That's right, Sun-joo."

She is bubbling again now.

"And we'll save up money and buy dresses like the embroidered ones you had in Pyongyang before they took your father away."

"They'll be the most beautiful dresses anyone ever wore, Sun-joo."

Suddenly the sparkle is gone from her eyes. I shiver. It mustn't be like this. I need her to keep making her jokes, to stay positive.

"Sun-joo, whatever is wrong?"

"I've got a bit of a problem I need to tell you about, princess."

I feel my stomach flip with anxiety. I realise straightaway what her problem is. I hardly need to say it.

"You can't swim, can you, Sun-joo?"

She looks irritated for a second, then she gives me a lopsided smile.

"No one ever taught me and I couldn't see the point, anyway. Until now, that is."

I know I am about to cry – something Sun-joo hates. If I ever weep, she feels she's failed me.

"Then we'll stay here in North Korea," I whisper. "It's not so terrible. Not now I've got you."

She shakes her head.

"Oh, it is terrible. It's about as terrible as it could possibly get. Which is why you will be swimming across that river tonight, if I have to throw you in the water myself."

She pulls me towards her and we hug. I don't know if I can bear it any more. If I cross the border, there will be no one in the world who will hold me like this. I can barely remember my mother, but my father and grandmother both loved to hug me. Soon there will be no one.

My face is wet with tears – my own and Sun-joo's. Finally she pushes me away from her.

She has never looked so serious.

"Don't you dare get shot, Hyun-mi. Don't drown. Don't do anything but survive. I know this is all for your father and grandmother, but escape for me too."

"I'll try," I say, "I promise."

Then she gives me a brave smile that I'll remember always.

"And don't forget to send a postcard. If you address it to the Dear Leader, I'm sure he'll see it gets passed on to me!"

GEORGIE

I'd told Omar I wasn't interested but he kept nagging me to watch it.

"You should see it, man. It's been on TV twice today already."

Secretly, I wasn't sure I could cope with the sight of my mum and dad pleading with me to come home.

"You can come round our place and look at it there. Fatima would love you to, you know that."

I pointed down at my grubby clothes.

"Look at the state of me, Omar. I haven't had a bath in weeks. I stink. I look disgusting."

He nodded.

"You do stink, man. No offence, but I can smell you from here. If you won't come round, you've got to find a shop or somewhere that's showing it."

***

Tired and cold, I leant against the glass front of a brightly-lit store that sold TVs and other electrical goods. I knew it wouldn't be long before a security man came out and shooed me off.

Almost all the televisions were tuned to the *Celebrity Skin* reality show. I could see Justin, the ex-singer of a once famous rock band, cavorting around in just a pair of tight gold trousers. He was beating his chest like an ape and making faces at the cameras. He might as well have been in a cage at the zoo.

A man in a dark blue uniform appeared as if on cue.

"Oi, kid! Move along will you? And don't

even think about dossing down in our doorway tonight, all right?

"It's supposed to be a free country," I said. "I'm not doing you any harm."

"You're bad for business, pal. Just move along or you'll get my boot up your backside."

I started moving off but called back over my shoulder.

"I don't suppose you could spare us some change?"

"You're right, I couldn't. Now get lost."

I shuffled, head down, past a seedy-looking pub and peered in through the windows. It was cheerless and almost empty, but the flickering television set above the bar had caught my eye. Then I saw them. My mum and dad were on the screen, sitting down in front of the journalists and press photographers.

I stepped inside the pub. A young barmaid was perched on a stool thumbing a text message into her mobile. She didn't even look up as I slipped into a dimly-lit alcove and sat down. She couldn't see me hiding in the shadows, but

I could see and hear the television.

Dad spoke first. He looked tired and stressed but he still knew how to use the media.

"Thanks for turning out today, folks," he said hoarsely. "I know a lot of you have got some strong opinions about me. But this isn't about politics. I'm not here today as the former leader of the British Fascist Party, I'm here as a father desperate to be reunited with his son."

The cameras flashed. Mum started sobbing into a screwed up tissue.

"I've made some mistakes in my life. But the biggest ones have cost me my relationship with the son I love."

He stopped addressing the journalists and turned to face the TV camera.

"Georgie, if you're watching, you need to know I've changed. I've not become some bearded, sandal-wearing left-winger, but you and your friends have made me think about the things I believe in and what I stand for. I wouldn't go back to the Party now, even if they'd have me. I no longer share their views."

He put his arm around my mum and pulled her closer to him.

"The most important thing, Georgie, is to get you back home. I'll do whatever it takes for that to happen."

"We love you, son, we miss you so much," Mum blurted tearfully.

The camera flashes exploded like fireworks.

I found that I was crying too.

The news report finished with a picture of me – in my school uniform, hair clean and combed. The face didn't look much like the images I'd been seeing reflected in shop windows. I left the pub unnoticed.

As I stepped onto the street, I heard Fatima's voice in my head.

I believe he has changed, Georgie - he's not the man he was. Isn't it time for you to go back home now?

I found myself nodding even though she was miles away.

Yes, Fatima, it's time.

I was sitting at a bus shelter, trying to decipher the graffiti, when his shiny new Range Rover pulled up. He didn't shut the door behind him, just jumped down onto the pavement and rushed towards me. He was wearing this sheepskin coat that I always said made him look like a dodgy football agent. When he pulled me to his chest, I breathed in the aftershave, the shower gel, the scent I always recognised as making him my dad.

I thought he might say, "Who loves ya?" I wondered if he'd tease me about the way *I* smelled. But he just held me close for a long time. A bus stopped beside the shelter and bored-looking people stared out at us. An old, white-haired couple got off and the bus drove away. Still he held on to me. Finally he spoke.

"I thought I'd lost you, son. I'll do whatever it takes to keep you now. I promise."

★★★

It was a long drive home. The heater was turned right up and my bones began to feel less cold. We talked and talked. A lot of what we said was heavy and emotional, but we laughed together too. As we neared our house I remembered something Omar had told me. It was Fatima's latest plan.

"You know you said you'd do anything to get me back home? Well, there's a favour I need to ask. It's not exactly a deal-breaker, but it would mean a lot to me if you'd come through on it."

He glanced across at me.

"Whatever you want, Georgie. If I have to go on TV and renounce fascism I'll do it. Though I guess I already did that today, didn't I?"

"I need you to pay for a plane ticket."

He nodded, eyes fixed on the road ahead.

"OK. Where do you want to go? Can we all come with you – make it a holiday?"

"It's not for me. It's for this girl who lives in South Korea. Originally, she's from North Korea but she escaped through China and now she's in the South. Her name's Hyun-mi."

I caught him smothering a grin with his hand.

"Hyun-mi, indeed. Did you meet her on the internet or something? Is she like a Thai bride?"

I didn't smile.

"She's a friend of Fatima's with an amazing story. And Fatima's making it her life's work to get it known by as many people as possible."

He rolled his lower lip.

"I thought what Fatima did to me in Cable Street was her life's work."

"Apparently not. She's on a new mission."

He took one hand off the steering wheel and patted the coat pocket where he carried his wallet.

"So all I've got to do is shell out for an air fare and you'll come home for good?"

"Yeah. Absolutely."

"Some people might find it ironic that I've spent so long trying to keep foreigners out of this country and now I'll be flying one in here. But. . ."

"Forget all that, Dad. Will you do it or not?"

He flicked on the indicator as we turned at last into our driveway.

"Consider it done, Georgie boy."

★★★

Later, I slid under the warm bathwater so that it covered my head, and blew a stream of bubbles to the surface. I'd needed two water changes and a lot of scrubbing to get myself clean. Outside the door, I could hear my mum fussing. I think she was worried I might climb out the bathroom window and disappear again.

"You all right, darling? You're going to dissolve if you stay in there much longer."

On the radiator she'd left a fluffy white bathrobe and my pyjamas. Perched near the taps were an empty bottle of Coke and a bowl that had once held five scoops of ice cream and some chocolate sauce.

"Can I get you anything else to eat? Just say the word."

My sister Albion, who I admit had seemed

delighted to see me, was getting irritable. Perhaps the novelty of having me here was wearing off.

"Is he ever coming out of there? I'm going round Lulu's and I need my make-up."

"Alb, he hasn't had a good long soak in ages. Anyway, I don't see why you have to get all made up just to go round your friend's."

"Mum, don't start, all right?"

It felt good to be home. I could hardly bear to tell them I'd be off again as soon as Hyun-mi got the documents so she could travel to England. I doubted it would take long. Fatima had contacts all over the world. And as I knew from Cable Street, Fatima could make the impossible happen.

HYUN-MI

For someone who'd never expected to leave North Korea, I'd become quite a traveller. Fatima had always promised that we'd meet one day and now I was jetting towards her.

I knew very little about London. I suppose I expected the same culture shock I'd had when I first reached South Korea's capital, Seoul. It had been impossible for me to take it in: the soaring, silver skyscrapers; giant, pulsing video screens; and, everywhere, restaurants serving mouth-watering food to people who'd never known hunger.

I don't want to sound ungrateful, but

South Korea was so fast-moving, so modern that I felt it was racing away from me and I'd never be able to catch up. The Dear Leader always claimed South Koreans were much worse off than us. But that was just another of his lies. Our cousins in the South were richer than I could have imagined. Though my family had been part of the elite in North Korea, I now felt like a poor relation.

The organisation that had got me out of China found a family for me to stay with in Seoul. They were kind, but a bit formal. I missed my dearest friend, Sun-joo, a free-spirit who had no time for rules and formalities. How guilty I felt that I was living in luxury. The best Sun-joo could hope for was to stay out of the prison camps.

Across the aisle of the plane, a stressed-out mother was trying to get her small son to eat the food the air hostess had brought. He was like an angel, with blonde hair and blue eyes. I hadn't seen many Europeans and I couldn't stop looking at him. Finally, he put a spoonful into his mouth, pulled a face then spat it out. I know he was only little but it made me so angry. I thought of street children in North Korea who spent whole days just grubbing for grains of rice in the dirt.

The mother caught my eye. She said something in English that I didn't understand. I just smiled back.

I picked up my bag from the carousel and walked out into the arrivals hall at London Heathrow. There seemed to be hundreds of people all staring at me. Some held signs that I couldn't read. I began to panic. Fatima had promised she'd be here to meet me, but which face was hers? Suddenly, her thought-voice was inside my head, bubbling like a clear mountain stream.

Hyun-mi, you're here at last. I've waited so long for this moment.

Ahead of me I saw her, a delicate looking girl in a headscarf. She was next to a skinny boy who I took to be her brother, Omar. He was waving and beckoning me towards them. It was only then I realised that Fatima could not see me.

I didn't know you were blind.

There are worse hardships, Hyun-mi. I consider myself a very lucky person, especially now you're here.

We hugged for a long time and I thought back to the day I'd swum across the Tumen River to freedom. Fatima had encouraged me onwards, away from the border guards' bullets. I remembered the long nights in China, curled up under a blanket in that half-finished building. Fatima's soothing words had been like a mother's lullaby to me. I'd always expected that I would cry if I ever did meet her. But I found instead that I was smiling.

We caught an underground train into London. The network went on endlessly with what seemed like hundreds of stops. In North Korea, my father and I had ridden once on Pyongyang's two-line metro. I thought of him and a wave of sorrow washed over me. How we would have loved to travel the world together.

I'd grown up in a country where everyone looked and thought pretty much the same. London was totally different. All colours and cultures were here. And the fashions! A warrior-like boy got into our carriage – he had metal rings dangling from his ears and nose, and studs in his forehead too. I just stared, mouth open, but no one else seemed to notice him.

A tall, smiley black man with a large woollen hat got on the train with his guitar just as the doors were closing. He played noisily and sang off-key. Again, nobody appeared to care. Try that on the Pyongyang Metro, I thought. You'd be dragged away and beaten by the police.

At last we reached our stop. Fatima took hold of my arm and we got up to leave. I smiled at her, though, of course, she could not see it.

I don't know how to thank you, Fatima.

She squeezed my hand.

Actually, Hyun-mi, there is something I'd like you to do...

MELISSA

"It's got to stop, girl!"

I clunked the fridge door shut so the kitchen was no longer lit by its little yellow bulb, but just by the moonlight from outside. When I turned, I saw his silhouette - a giant with a tangle of dreadlocks. For a big guy, he'd done a pretty good job of sneaking up on me.

"You stalking me or something?" I asked.

He switched on the overhead light and I laughed out loud. TJ was built like a weightlifter but he was wearing my mum's pink dressing-gown. On him, it was like a miniskirt.

"Looking good, TJ."

He tried to keep his serious face on, as if we were father and daughter.

"TJ, I'll give you a million pounds if you go out the flat dressed like that."

He couldn't help it. He started laughing too.

"Melissa, it ain't funny, really. It's disrespectful to your mum, apart from anything else. She's told you to stop taking stuff from behind her back and you keep doing it."

I looked down at the floor. The carrier bag I'd scooped some pies and other things into dangled by my side.

"I was just hungry, TJ. I wake up sometimes and I feel like I'm going to die if I don't get something to eat."

He moved over to the kitchen table and pulled out a chair for me. Then he walked round so he could sit opposite.

"You're like the police now, TJ. You going to read me my rights, or something?"

He shook his big head. His dreadlocks looked like dusty pieces of rope.

"I want to help you, girl. Really. See, I take

a lot of pride in how I look now – I'm always working out and everything. But when I was your age, I was a bit, you know, chubby. I loved my food. What I'm trying to say is, I understand what you're going through."

"No disrespect, Teej, but you're not my dad, OK?"

He looked down at his big, meaty hands.

"That's true, Melissa, but your mum and I have been talking. . ."

He glanced up at me as though he was trying to catch my thoughts. TJ was desperate for my mum to marry him.

"I wouldn't get your hopes up. She's had a billion boyfriends before you and not one of them made it down the aisle with her."

The moment I said it, I wished I hadn't. Remember, this was the new, improved Melissa, not the mean, old version.

"Could I just take these few bits of food? It's probably best if I don't cut down all at once."

He nodded and his dreadlocks bounced

up and down.

"OK, Melissa. Like I say, I care about you. I'm just trying to help."

I don't know why I did it. Probably I was just trying to get him off my case. But I leant forward and kissed him on the cheek.

"Thanks, Teej. Goodnight, yeah?"

Suddenly, the room was lit up by his hundred watt smile. It was like this was one of the all-time happiest moments in his life.

"Yeah, right. Goodnight, Melissa," he said. "Sleep tight, OK?"

I stopped in the doorway.

"You know I'm going to be the bridesmaid at my learning support assistant Stacey's wedding? Maybe I'll get another chance to wear that dress."

I left him rocking back on his chair and chuckling happily to himself.

★★★

I waited half an hour. By now I could hear TJ

snoring through the wall – he sounded like a walrus or something dozing after ten buckets of fish. How my mum put up with that? Finally, I slipped out of our place and crept along the balconies and walkways to the burnt-out flat where Georgie had been staying before he went back home.

I tapped on the boarded-up window.

"Wake up, Jack. I brought you something to eat."

GEORGIE

When the train arrived at the station in Docklands, Fatima was standing on the platform with the last person in the world I wanted to see. She looked small and frail, holding the sleeve of his jacket and smiling up at him. It was as though everything he'd done to us, all the fear he'd caused us, was forgotten.

"What's he doing here, Fatima?" I said, by way of a greeting.

Jack looked down at his shoes.

"I'd like you to meet our new Street Hero!" Fatima said.

I just laughed.

"How can he be one of us? He's not been through what we've been through together."

"He has the gift. That's all that matters."

"But he terrorised us, Fatima. I can't forgive him for that."

She rarely looked angry, but a flash of annoyance passed across her features.

"Jack is sorry for his past. He wants to make it up to us. It's not that long ago, Georgie, that you were our enemy, remember?"

I shrugged.

"It just seems too soon. How do we know we can trust him?"

"How do I know I can trust you?"

"Oh, Fatima. Give it a rest."

"Jack can be very useful to us, Georgie."

With his big shoulders and boxer's hands, I could see that Jack might add some grit and muscle to our crew.

"So you've restyled yourself as Fatima's bodyguard, Jack? Who'd have thought it?"

He grunted. He still wouldn't look me in the eye.

"I'm trying to make things right, Georgie. Don't push it, hey?"

Fatima began to cluck like a mother hen.

"Come along, boys. It really is time you both looked to the future. Imagine what we can achieve if we all work together."

I imagined myself landing a beautiful punch on that ugly, squashed hooter of his. He glared at me. Clearly he'd read my mind. I decided to ignore him for now.

"Are we meeting the others near the compound?" I asked

"They're in position already."

"Then let's go."

They were waiting in a dingy alley, looking very suspicious. Melissa had this beanie hat pulled down low over her face. She was wearing a black puffa jacket and Ugg-type boots. She looked like a commando. Omar was also wearing dark clothes. The Korean girl with them looked bemused.

"Don't worry about Hyun-mi," Fatima said. "She's done much braver things than this."

We compared cover stories – the lies we'd told to get out of our houses for the night. Fatima hated deceit, but she said our noble mission meant we were justified.

"Who's got the step ladder?" I asked.

Jack swung the pack he was carrying off his shoulder.

"It's a rope ladder and I've got it."

Melissa giggled.

"Am I going to be all right on a rope ladder?"

Jack gave her a ragged smile.

"It's a heavy-duty one. You should be fine."

★★★

We waited around for ages. Fatima said we should give the inhabitants of the *Celebrity Skin* house time to go to bed. She wanted the security guards to be half asleep too. So, at three o'clock in the morning, I finally started to climb the perimeter wall of the compound where the show was filmed. It must have been frightening for Fatima to climb over that wall but she didn't complain. Melissa got stuck and just hung there squealing. How no one heard us coming I'll never know.

The way Fatima had described it, her plan sounded simple: break in to the *Celebrity Skin* house, grab a microphone and broadcast to the nation. OK, it sounded certain to fail, but it was Fatima's plan and she'd convinced us it would work.

"Was I right about Cable Street?" she kept asking.

Finally, all six of us were standing on the damp grass inside the compound. We could see lights on in the house where the celebrities lived, but no one stirred. Fatima wanted us to find a place to hide for a while. She had it in her mind that we'd try and take over the airwaves at 8 p.m., peak viewing time, when *Celebrity Skin* got its biggest audience of the day.

I was just thinking how hard it would be

to stay hidden in a place with so many cameras when I heard a cough from behind some potted plants. The tip of a cigarette glowed red, then a figure stepped out of the darkness.

"Evening all," he said.

MELISSA

I screamed when I saw him. Not because he's famous but because he just appeared out of nowhere. He was wearing this big coat that must have belonged to one of the security guards. On his feet he had flip flops even though it was minus fifty degrees or something. He had these skintight trousers made from shiny gold material. His hair was really long and wavy, like a girl's, and he had these fleshy lips that kept moving and twitching.

The smoke from his cigarette was blowing into his eyes. He screwed them up but carried on looking at us. Finally, he stepped forward with his hand stretched out. We all took turns to shake it, even Jack, who kept glaring at him, daring him to try something.

"I'm Justin," he said, though we all knew that, of course. "Pleased to meet you. I hope you're a bit more interesting than those muppets in the house. To be honest, they're boring me to tears."

He pointed with a thumb to where the other celebrities were sleeping.

"There are smoke detectors everywhere indoors. I have to come out here for a fag, even though it's freezing."

Apart from the borrowed coat, his gold trousers seemed to be the only clothes he was wearing.

"Are you fans of the show or something?"

I started to say that I was, but Fatima shook her head.

"I'll be honest with you, Justin, we need to ask you a favour. We plan to hijack *Celebrity Skin* later today and broadcast a message to the nation. We think people should be ashamed of themselves for tuning in to this ridiculous strip show – no offence, but you're all just attention-seekers. We'll tell the audience they should use their brains more and find out what's going on in the real world."

Justin took another long drag on his cigarette. I felt a bit sorry for him because Fatima was basically saying that he was part of the problem she wanted to solve. Finally, he tossed his hair back out of his eyes and flicked his cigarette butt into some bushes.

"It sounds like a brilliant idea. Count me in."

GEORGIE

A whole day in a cleaner's cupboard with Hyun-mi and Fatima might just have been bearable. But having Melissa, Omar and Jack in there too was a total wind-up. It was cramped and stuffy. Fortunately, there was a camera-free toilet right next door.

At least we didn't make much noise. Talking out loud could have given us away, so we only used our thought-voices.

Finally Justin leant through the door and pointed to his watch.

"It's show-time, darlings!" he said.

He pressed the radio microphone he'd

been wearing into Fatima's hands.

"Speak into this. They'll hear you better."

Now there was no need to sneak around. We just followed him along the corridors to the main living area where most of the cameras were.

When we entered, several people screamed. Someone in the kitchen dropped a saucepan.

"Oh my god, what's going on?" cried a pop star I sort of recognised, who was standing by the window in a leopard-skin bikini.

Apart from Justin, all the celebrities were calling for help. At any moment, I expected security guards to charge in and wrestle us to the ground.

Our minds were all buzzing. Kids like us with the gift were sending out thought-waves saying they could see us on their television screens. What was happening? What were we playing at?

A deeply tanned soap actor was shrieking at Justin.

"I can't believe you knew about this. I feel betrayed, Justin. You've put us all in danger."

"Leave Justin alone," Jack hissed, "or I'll punch your lights out."

The soap actor retreated with his hands up by his face.

Outside the windows of the *Celebrity Skin* house, I could see uniformed security guards moving like sharks in an unlit tank. Some pressed their noses right up against the glass. They were glaring at us, and one was shouting into a walkie-talkie, but they made no move to come into the living area.

That's when I realised that nobody was going to stop us. For the programme makers watching in the control room, this was just more publicity for their show. They didn't want the security guards to drag us away – not yet anyway. It would be all over the newspapers tomorrow – a bunch of kids had broken in to the *Celebrity Skin* house. Imagine that!

At last, everyone quietened down. They were all looking at Fatima. Wasn't she familiar?

Hadn't they seen this skinny blind girl before somewhere?

"So, kids," Justin announced. "It's ten past eight. Would you like to broadcast your message to the world now?"

I could hear Melissa whispering urgently.

"Fatima, yeah, please don't tell people they can never watch this sort of show. Say it should be educational stuff as well as *Celebrity Skin*. A bit of both, yeah?"

Fatima smiled then called my name softly. I took her arm and pointed her towards one of the cameras that was fixed to a wall. It moved slightly and I watched its robot eye zoom in on her.

She coughed, then began to address the millions who were watching in a strong, clear voice.

"You know who we are, or you should do. We're the Street Heroes. A while ago, we had a message for the British Fascist Party when they tried to march down Cable Street. Now we've got something to say to all of you.

"These game shows, soap operas, talent contests. . . I suppose there's a place for them."

Melissa was nodding.

"But there's so much more to life. Maybe because I can't actually see television, I don't get it. It seems to me, though, that it's only doing half its job. Yes, it entertains you, if you don't mind having your brain turned to mush. But shouldn't it be telling you what's really going on in the world, inspiring you to change things for the better? Please think about what I'm saying. Please open your minds."

She spoke like a real star. Justin started to clap theatrically, but the other celebrities simply gawped at her.

I nudged Hyun-mi. She stepped closer to Fatima and they linked arms like sisters who'd known each other a lifetime.

"Anyway, enough of me. There's someone else I want to introduce to you this evening. She comes from a very strange and frightening country called North Korea. Her name's Hyun-mi and she's got this amazing story. . ."

About the story

I made a lot of programmes when I was a TV reporter, but the one I'm most proud of was about a strange and frightening country called North Korea. Journalists are not allowed to visit, so to go there I had to pretend to be one of the very few tourists they let in each year. I felt uncomfortable all the time I was in North Korea, but, as a Westerner, I think they'd just have thrown me out if they'd known what I was up to. Another journalist who worked on the programme put himself in much greater danger. He secretly filmed the many street children in North Korea left to starve by its ruler Kim Jong-il. The so-called 'Dear Leader' claims to love all the children in his country, but he has allowed many thousands of them to die while he spends his country's resources on nuclear weapons and North Korea's massive army.

The brave journalist who worked with our
Channel Four team was a young North Korean who
I knew as Ahn Chol. That wasn't his real name –
to protect himself and others, he kept his identity
secret. His parents had died in one of North Korea's
many famines but he'd managed to escape
over the border into China.
Ahn Chol decided to go back into North Korea
undercover to film the street children who were
suffering so badly. If he'd been caught by the police,
he would have been arrested and killed.
The programme we made was called *Children of the
Secret State*. This book is dedicated to Ahn Chol,
who risked his life to bring their story to the world.

Joe Layburn

Joe Layburn has spent most of his life in
East London. His dad thought it would be
fantastic for Joe and his three brothers to grow up
surrounded by the fresh air and green fields
of the country but Joe missed London and
moved back as soon as he could.

Joe was a TV reporter and journalist for
15 years before becoming a teacher.
He has always loved writing stories and the
modern and historical East End is
a big inspiration for him.

Joe lives in East London with his wife
Marianne and three sons, Richie, Charlie and Hal.
Joe and his sons are season-ticket holders at
West Ham football club. His other books
for Frances Lincoln are *Street Heroes* and *Ghostscape*.